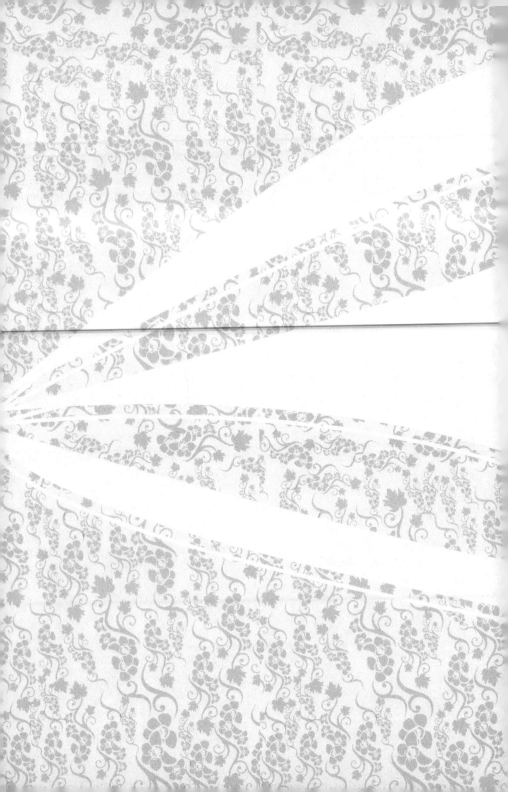

BEACH BLUES

BY DIANA G. GALLAGHER
illustrated by Brann Garvey

Librarian Reviewer
Laurie K. Holland
Media Specialist (National Board Certified), Edina, MN
MA in Elementary Education, Minnesota State University, Mankato

Reading Consultant
Sherry Klehr
Elementary/Middle School Educator, Edina Public Schools, MN
MA in Education, University of Minnesota

STONE ARCH BOOKS
www.stonearchbooks.com

Claudia Cristina Cortez is published by Stone Arch Books,
A Capstone Imprint
1710 Roe Crest Drive
North Mankato, Minnesota 56003
www.capstonepub.com

Library of Congress Cataloging-in-Publication Data
Gallagher, Diana G.
  Beach Blues: The Complicated Life of Claudia Cristina Cortez / by Diana
G. Gallagher; illustrated by Brann Garvey.
     p. cm. — (Claudia Cristina Cortez)
  ISBN 978-1-4342-0773-9 (library binding)
  ISBN 978-1-4342-0869-9 (pbk.)
  [1. Vacations—Fiction. 2. Family reunions—Fiction. 3. Babysitters—
Fiction. 4. Interpersonal relations—Fiction. 5. Hispanic Americans—Fiction.]
I. Garvey, Brann, ill. II. Title.
PZ7.G13543Be 2009
[Fic]—dc22   2008004284

Summary: Claudia's family is on vacation. So why is she stuck babysitting her
three younger cousins?

Art Director: Heather Kindseth
Graphic Designer: Kay Fraser

Photo Credits
Delaney Photography, cover, 1

Printed in the United States of America in Stevens Point, Wisconsin.
042013
007349R

Table of Contents

Cast of

ME

CLAUDIA

That's me. I'm thirteen, and I'm in the seventh grade at Pine Tree Middle School. I live with my mom, my dad, and my brother, Jimmy. I have one cat, Ping-Ping. I like music, baseball, and hanging out with my friends.

RANDI

RANDI lives in Florida. She's in the same grade that I am. She loves snorkeling, playing volleyball, and eating hot dogs. She and her brother, Mason, live in a house near the motel where my family is staying in Florida.

MASON

MASON is Randi's big brother. He's in eighth grade. He's really nice! He loves watching movies and playing dominoes. He told me that his favorite food is hamburgers. We have a lot of fun together!

MOM is the person who makes sure we all do what we're supposed to. On vacation, she plans meals, organizes sightseeing, and helps with cooking.

MOM

Characters

DAD is usually boring. That's why it's a big surprise that he planned a trip to Florida for us!

JIMMY is my big brother. He's obsessed with videogames and computers. He doesn't talk to me very much, except when I do something to annoy him. I usually try to stay out of his way, but sometimes he helps me out.

UNCLE DIEGO is my dad's brother. He spends a lot of time at our house. I really like Uncle Diego. He treats me like a grownup and always gives me good advice. He likes playing the guitar and eating sandwiches.

GRANDMA is my favorite person in the whole world. She teaches me big words and we read books together. She lives near us, so I see her at least once a week.

Cast of

ALISHA is my seven-year-old cousin. She's always crabby and never smiles. As far as I can tell, the only thing she really likes to do is complain about everything.

JOSE is Alisha's six-year-old brother. He likes watching TV. He's also obsessed with pirates. If Jose isn't watching cartoons, he is trying to figure out a way to watch cartoons.

GABE is Alisha and Jose's three-year-old brother. The only thing Gabe likes to do is cry. He's pretty cute, but he's always getting into my stuff and wrecking things.

AUNT MARIA and UNCLE RENALDO arc Alisha, Jose, and Gabe's parents. Aunt Maria is Dad's sister.

Characters

GREAT-AUNT LOUISA and **GREAT-UNCLE SAM** don't have any kids. Great-Uncle Sam is Grandma's brother.

GREAT-AUNT LOUISA

GREAT-UNCLE SAM

GREAT-GRANDPA is Grandma and Great-Uncle Sam's father. He's turning 85, and we're going to Florida to celebrate his birthday!

GREAT-GRANDPA

BRAD TURINO is the guy I like at school. He's a star on the football team. He's also a really, really nice guy.

BRAD

CHAPTER 1

Tuesday
Surprise

My father is **dependable** and boring. He wears a suit and goes to work before I get up, six days a week. He comes home at 6:15 **every night**. Then he reads the newspaper, eats dinner, watches TV, and goes to bed.

He does that **every day** except Sunday. Dad's computer store is closed on Sunday, but he still gets up **early**. He reads the newspaper in the morning. Then he works around the house and watches sports on TV.

Every Sunday.

Today wasn't Sunday. It was Tuesday. When I went to the kitchen, Dad was at the breakfast table reading the newspaper.

I stopped and stared. I was too **surprised** to talk. It was as **shocking** as if a **T. rex** had just squashed our kitchen.

Dad looked at his watch. "It's after eight," he said. "Aren't you *late* for school?"

"No school," I said. I was on winter break, but Dad doesn't take breaks. "What's wrong?" I asked.

My **mom** handed me a glass of orange juice. "Sit down, Claudia," she said. "Your father has something to tell you."

My throat closed up. I thought that something terrible must have happened. "Am I failing math?" I asked. "Are we moving? Did someone die?" I gasped. "Is something wrong with Grandma?"

"Well, she's going away for a while," Dad said.

"She can't!" I exclaimed. **Grandma** understood me. She listened to me, and she almost never yelled. She was always FAIR, even when I did something AWFUL and didn't deserve it.

"I'll miss her," I said sadly.

"You'll have **plenty of time** with her," Dad said. "It's a long drive to Florida."

Mom smiled. I frowned.

My older brother, **Jimmy**, walked in and rolled his eyes. "Don't remind me," he said.

I blinked. "Is Jimmy going to Florida?" I asked.

"We're all going," Dad said. "To the Gulf of Mexico. With Grandma."

"And Aunt Maria's family," Mom added. "Your Great-Grandpa Cortez will be eighty-five next Sunday. We're celebrating his birthday on the beach. We'll have a **big party**."

"When are we leaving?" I asked.

"First thing tomorrow," Dad answered.

"**WOO-HOO!**" I shrieked. I jumped out of my chair. "I've got to pack!" I yelled.

"One suitcase per person," Dad said.

"Okay!" I said. I ran upstairs to my room, but I didn't start packing. First, I took a new spiral notebook out of my desk.

I'd never been to Florida or seen the Gulf of Mexico. I wanted to write everything down.

I opened the notebook to the first page and wrote:

Claudia's Fabulous Florida Vacation Journal

I turned to the next page and wrote:

Market Street. Tuesday, 8:14 a.m.

I love vacations! No school, and no chores! Just fun!

My To Do List

PACK!

Tell friends I'm leaving

Say goodbye to Ping-Ping

Jimmy was ready to leave in fifteen minutes. He packed his video games first. They almost filled up his suitcase. He stuffed clothes in the empty spaces. He was bringing three t-shirts, two pair of shorts, a bathing suit, underwear, and flip-flops.

"That's **not enough clothes** for a week," I said.

"We're going to the beach," Jimmy explained. "All I need is a bathing suit."

That made sense, but I wanted to be ready for
ANYTHING.

I put my favorite outfits in the washer.
Then I helped Mom make sandwiches and
pack snacks for the car.

"There must be something I don't like about
vacations," I said. "But I can't think of anything."

"Sunscreen!" Mom exclaimed.

"I love sunscreen," I said. "I'd rather be slippery
than sunburned."

"Get it now so we don't forget," Mom said. "I'll
check the laundry."

I found two tubes of sunscreen in the bathroom.
I took them downstairs and slipped them into my
suitcase.

Then Dad walked in, carrying a big plastic cat
carrier. "Come on, Claudia," he said. "We've got to
take Ping-Ping to the vet."

My cat hates going to the vet when we're gone. I
hate taking her, but *someone has to feed her.*

I wish I could explain that to her, but I don't speak cat. Ping-Ping probably thinks I'm **never coming back.**

Claudia's Fabulous Florida Vacation Journal

Market Street. Tuesday, 3:37 p.m.

I thought of two things I don't like about going on vacation: feeling guilty about leaving my cat and missing my friends. I promised to send postcards to Becca and Monica, my best friends.

Packing List

I put everything I couldn't live without on my bed. The pile was a lot bigger than my suitcase. So I packed the most important stuff first.

Clothes: bathing suit, shorts, tops, jeans, sandals, pajamas, a skirt, a sweater, sweats, underwear, and socks.

Bathroom supplies: toothpaste, toothbrush, comb, brush, and shampoo with conditioner. And my Pearly Pink lip gloss stick.

Books: Two new books, to read if I'm bored (or if it's raining).

Beach gear: sunglasses, flip-flops, hat, beach towel, snorkel, goggles, and fins.

Flashlight.

The latest issues of my favorite **magazines.**

I flipped the top of my suitcase over, but I couldn't zip it closed. **It was too full!**

I couldn't leave my swimming stuff behind. **I was going to the beach!**

I needed my books and magazines, and I needed my flashlight so I could read under the covers.

I absolutely had to have my bathroom supplies. Besides, they didn't take up much room. But **something had to go.**

Jimmy was right. We wouldn't need a lot of clothes at the beach. I kept my flip-flops, jeans, and sweater, but I took out the sandals, skirt, and sweats. I had to sit on my suitcase and 𝓑𝓞𝓤𝓝𝓒𝓔 to smash things down. I **finally** got it closed.

Claudia's Fabulous Florida Vacation Journal

Market Street. Tuesday, 10:10 p.m.

I can't sleep. It's too quiet, and I'm too excited. My dad isn't as boring as I thought he was. We're going to Florida!

CHAPTER 2

Wednesday

Hitting the Road

Uncle Diego slept at our house. He was already awake when I got up. He helped my dad load the car. Then we headed to Grandma's house.

When we got there, **Grandma wasn't ready.**

"It's after eight, Mom," Dad said.

"I know," **Grandma** said. She smiled and went back inside.

Dad can hurry up Mom, Jimmy, Uncle Diego, and me, but he can't rush Grandma.

Grandma came back with two suitcases.

"You can only bring one," Dad said.

"I need two," Grandma said.

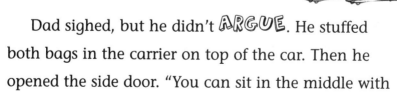

Dad sighed, but he didn't 𝔸ℝ𝔾𝕌𝔼. He stuffed both bags in the carrier on top of the car. Then he opened the side door. "You can sit in the middle with Claudia," Dad told Grandma.

Uncle Diego and Jimmy were in back. Mom sat up front with Dad.

"After I use the bathroom," Grandma said. She went back inside.

Dad checked his watch. **He tapped his foot and sighed**, but he didn't argue.

Claudia's Fabulous Florida Vacation Journal

Grandma's House. Wednesday, 8:13 a.m.

When you're old, nobody makes you wait to use a bathroom.

Driving Me Crazy

Road trips can be fun or boring. Long drives with my family are a little bit of both.

Mom and Dad don't like teenager music. So I started learning the words to old rock-and-roll songs. That was fun. **Until the station got fuzzy.**

" . . . do-wah ditty ditty dum . . . ZZZZZZZZZZZZZZZ!"

"Static AGAIN?" I yelled, throwing up my hands. We had to find a new station every fifteen minutes. "Let's listen to my Bad Dog CD," I suggested. **Bad Dog** is my **all-time favorite** band.

"I'll find something," **Dad** said.

"We wouldn't lose the station if we had satellite radio," Jimmy said. He's a high-tech **expert**.

"Why should I pay for something I can get for free?" Dad asked.

"Right now, you're only getting five seconds of music for free. Then you get FUZZ. You get five seconds of twenty different stations for free," Uncle Diego said. He rubbed his nose and closed his eyes.

Finally, my dad got a music station on the radio. Uncle Diego started SNORING.

I started feeling bored. My mom could read in the car, but it always made me **sick to my stomach.** I looked for license plates and wrote the states down in my journal. I dozed off. I was tired after being up late the night before. But I only slept a few minutes. Then I ate a sandwich and drank a soda.

Dad stopped at a rest area when Grandma had to go. Just in time, too. **I was about to burst!**

When we got in the car again, Grandma asked, "Who wants to play the alphabet game?"

"Can we use **any letter** we see?" Uncle Diego asked.

"Only letters that begin a word or stand alone," Grandma said. "And no license plates. **That's the rule.** It's not fun if it's too easy."

Uncle Diego went back to sleep.

Grandma and I played the alphabet game all the way through. TWICE.

Claudia's Fabulous Florida Vacation Journal

Interstate 75, somewhere in Georgia. Wednesday, 5:12 p.m.

We just keep driving and driving and driving. On an endless road that never gets out of Georgia!

Dad stopped at a motel with a restaurant. It was just after dark. We were all **starved**, but he wanted to get our rooms first.

"We'll RELAX and EAT," Dad said. "Then we'll get a good night's sleep."

I had a **grilled cheese sandwich** and fries at the restaurant. Then we went to our rooms. Dad, Uncle Diego, and Jimmy shared one room. Mom, Grandma, and I had another. Grandma and Mom watched the news on TV. I read another chapter of my book.

Claudia's Fabulous Florida Vacation Journal

Interstate 75, somewhere in Florida. Wednesday, 9:47 p.m.

Motel pillows are too squishy.

CHAPTER 3

Thursday
Blue Dolphin

The morning drive went fast. Mom and I sang **silly old songs.** Grandma helped me look for license plates. We had **18 states** when we arrived at our motel in Florida.

We stopped at a place called **The Blue Dolphin Motel**. It was right on the beach. I couldn't see the Gulf of Mexico from the parking lot. The swimming pool and a snack shack were in the way. The snack shack was built on a wide deck.

"Is the snack shack roof made of palm tree leaves?" I asked.

"They're called **FRONDS**," Grandma said. She never missed a chance to teach me a new word.

We walked past the snack shack and toward the beach. I gasped when I saw the water. **The Gulf of Mexico was huge!**

The waves were small, but the water stretched all the way to the horizon. I couldn't wait to get in it.

I kicked off my shoes and socks. I started to walk. But the sand was **burning hot!** I ran and jumped into the water. It felt fantastic on my sizzling feet.

I waded in the surf for a few minutes. Then Dad called me back to unpack.

I didn't have to share a room with Grandma. She was staying in a beach house with Great-Grandpa Cortez, Great-Aunt Louisa, and Great-Uncle Sam.

I wasn't sharing a room with Mom and Dad, either. Or with Uncle Diego and Jimmy.

I was STUCK with my three little cousins.

Aunt Maria and Uncle Renaldo have three kids, **Alisha, Jose, and Gabe**. I had to watch them last Thanksgiving while Aunt Maria, Mom, and Grandma made dinner. Those three cousins are on my Things I Can't Stand list.

Claudia's Things I Can't Stand List

1. Getting a cavity filled

2. My cousins

3. Splinters

"Mom!" **Alisha**, who was seven, YELLED when I walked in. "Claudia's getting wet sand all over our room!"

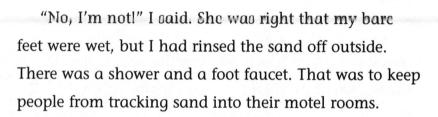

"No, I'm not!" I said. She was right that my bare feet were wet, but I had rinsed the sand off outside. There was a shower and a foot faucet. That was to keep people from tracking sand into their motel rooms.

Alisha stuck her tongue out. She was SPOILED and SNOTTY. I couldn't stand her.

There was a bathroom between our room and Aunt Maria's room. Alisha BANGED on her mom's door. Her mom didn't answer.

Jose turned up the volume on the TV. He was six. He never said or did much. He just watched cartoons.

My suitcase was on one of the beds. Someone had opened it. I sighed and walked over to the bed.

Something rattled on the floor.

I rushed over and looked down. Three-year-old **Gabe** was playing with my bathroom stuff.

"Those are mine," I said. Gabe wasn't mean like Alisha or weird like Jose. He was just the youngest. So he thought he could have everything he wanted.

"Mine," Gabe told me. He bit the end off my lip gloss.

"No!" I yelled. I took the case out of his hand. Only a little bit of gloss was left. **It was covered with little kid germs.**

Gabe spit out the glob of gloss. *Then he started to cry.*

"Shut up, Gabe!" Alisha yelled, covering her ears.

Jose didn't say anything. He just turned up the sound on the TV.

I gave Gabe my swim goggles. He chewed on the strap and stopped crying.

"Is this a good book?" Alisha asked. She was sitting on the bed, next to my suitcase. She picked up my book and opened it.

"Yes," I told her. "Don't lose my place!"
I didn't speak fast enough. My bookmark fell out.

"It can't be that good. *There aren't any pictures,*"
Alisha told me. She threw the book back in my
suitcase.

"Leave my stuff alone, okay?" I asked quietly.
I bent over to pick up my bathroom things.

Alisha stuck my snorkel in her mouth. YUCK!

"Mine!" Gabe yelled. He reached for the snorkel.
Alisha held it out of reach. Gabe SCREAMED.

Jose turned up the TV again.

I gave Alisha one of my magazines and let Gabe
have the snorkel. Then I turned the TV down.

Then Jose turned the sound up again. **Louder**.

Claudia's Fabulous Florida Vacation Journal

Motel Room, Florida. Thursday, 1:38 p.m.

I'm not unpacking. I used the little lock that
came with my suitcase to keep my stuff safe.

Then I hid the key. Maybe Grandma will buy
me another lip gloss.

After I locked my suitcase, I put my **flip-flops** on and headed outside.

"Mom told us to stay in the room," Alisha said. She folded her arms and GLARED at me.

"She told you and your brothers to stay," I said. "Not me!" I started walking.

"I'm telling!" Alisha yelled after me.

A few doors down, Mom and Dad's door was open. "I'm going to the beach house," I told them. "To see if Grandma needs anything."

They were still unpacking. **Mom** smiled. She said, "Okay," and waved.

I took off. I ran past a house with a blue door. The table on the deck had a blue umbrella. The Greats were staying in the next house. It had a big porch and a BBQ grill. **Great-Grandpa** was sitting at a picnic table. My great-aunt and great-uncle were sitting in the porch swing.

I don't have as many relatives as some kids do. Grandma has one brother, Great-Uncle Sam. Mom has a sister. She has two kids. But this was a Cortez family vacation.

Great-Grandpa Cortez walked with a cane. He had trouble remembering, so he lived with other old people. He had helpers who made sure he took his medicine and didn't forget to eat.

"There's Claudia!" Great-Grandpa called. He smiled and waved. *He never forgot me.*

Grandma came out the door. She was carrying glasses of **pink lemonade** on a tray.

"Thank you, Myra," Great-Aunt Louisa said. She fanned herself and took a glass. "I'm parched."

"Can I help with anything, Grandma?" I asked.

"No, but thanks for asking," **Grandma** said. "Go have some fun."

I raced toward the water. I couldn't go swimming without an adult, but I could wade and look for pretty shells.

Claudia's Fabulous Florida Vacation Journal

Seminole Beach, Florida. Thursday, 2:25 p.m.

Having fun in Florida will be easy. As long as I don't go back to my motel room. It's infested with cousins.

Buddies and Brats

At the beach, I saw two kids — a girl and a boy — riding the waves on **boogie boards**. Boogie boards look like cut-off surfboards. You hold on and let the water carry you onto the beach.

The boy had short dark hair and a nice smile. When he got off his board, he saw me watching and walked over. The girl followed him. She had a nice smile too. I guessed that they were brother and sister. They looked friendly.

"Want to try boogie boarding?" the **boy** asked, smiling.

"No thanks. I don't have my bathing suit on," I said. "And I don't want to be in the ocean ALONE."

"You won't be alone," the **girl** said. "Mason and I use **the buddy system**."

"Maybe later," I said. "Are you guys on vacation?"

"No, we live here," Mason said. He pointed to the house with the blue door, next door to where Grandma was staying.

They sat down and we talked. Randi was in seventh grade, just like me. Mason was in eighth. Their school was on **winter break** too. That meant we could hang out together.

I told them about **burning my feet on the sand.** "Does anything else on the beach hurt?" I asked nervously. I'd read about 𝒮𝒯ℐ𝒩𝒢ℐ𝒩𝒢 jellyfish and 𝐬𝐡𝐚𝐫𝐤𝐬. I did not want to see any up close.

"Don't feed the seagulls," Mason said.

"Why would that hurt?" I asked.

"They'll dive bomb you to get more," Randi explained.

"They don't 𝐟𝐥𝐲 𝐚𝐰𝐚𝐲 when you wave your arms," Mason said. "They think you're throwing more food."

"Hey, do you like miniature golf?" Randi asked me.

"**Love it!**" I said.

"Cool," Randi said. "You should come with us. We're going this afternoon!"

Then Randi and Mason's mother called them in. I went with them to meet her.

"Mom, can Claudia go with us to **Pirate's Cove?**" Randi asked.

"That's the miniature golf course," Mason told me.

"If it's okay with her parents," Mrs. Baker said. "Claudia, you can tell your mom and dad that Pirate's Cove is just a short walk down the beach."

As fast as I could, I ran back to the motel to ask my mom and dad if I could go. **I was so excited.** It was great luck to meet Randi and Mason! It was going to be a fantastic vacation!

Mom and Dad were sitting on a bench outside the motel with Aunt Maria and Uncle Renaldo. **Gabe** was playing in the sand. I ran up to them. I was *out of breath* when I finally stopped.

"Can I go play miniature golf down the beach at Pirate's Cove with my new friends?" I asked in my sweetest voice. "Their mom said it was okay," I added. "They live right there!" I pointed at Mason and Randi's house.

"PIRATES!" Jose yelled. He appeared in the doorway. "Is Pirate's Cove the place that has a ship and a skull cave? I want to go!"

I stared at Jose. I've never heard him talk so much before. I guess he **really likes pirates**.

"Me go, too!" Gabe shouted. Then he dumped a pail of sand on his head.

"Go where?" Alisha shouted from inside.

"To play pirate golf," Jose said.

"I don't want to play stupid golf," **Alisha** said, sticking her head out the window.

"Good," I said. **"You're not invited."**

"I want to go!" Jose insisted.

"Nobody is going to play golf," Dad said.

I gasped. "Why not?" I asked.

Mom explained, "Dad and I are going to buy groceries. The beach house has a kitchen. We'll all be eating over there. Aunt Maria and Uncle Renaldo are going shopping with us. *You have to watch your cousins.*"

"Why can't Jimmy or Uncle Diego watch them?" I asked.

Mom gave me a look. "Uncle Diego's taking a nap, and **Jimmy doesn't pay attention**," she told me.

I had to babysit. PERIOD. No way out.

When Randi came to get me, I told her the bad news. She was DISAPPOINTED, but she understood.

"Come over after dinner," Randi said. "We'll play dominoes. It's **more fun** with three."

"I'll be there!" I exclaimed.

Time drags when you're stuck in a motel room with my cousins.

Jose turned on cartoons and sobbed. Alisha locked herself in the bathroom, and Gabe poured wet sand on my pillow.

Claudia's Fantastic Florida Vacation Journal

Motel Room, Florida. Thursday, 4:47 p.m.

Why I shouldn't be upset about missing miniature golf:

1. I've played miniature golf before.

2. I'll see Randi and Mason later.

3. Someone has to watch the little kids.

But Uncle Diego and Jimmy and Great-Uncle Sam and Great-Aunt Louisa could babysit too. So how come I always get stuck with the three terrible tots?

CHAPTER 4

Later Thursday
Beach Feast

My whole family LOVES to eat. Our first meal at the beach was a banquet!

First Course: chips, dip, vegetable sticks, cheese squares

Second Course: tossed green salad, macaroni salad, olives

Third Course: hamburgers, beans, hot dogs, corn-on-the-cob, fries

Fourth Course: strawberry shortcake

The table at the beach house wasn't big enough for everyone. Uncle Diego and Jimmy sat on the porch swing. I sat on the steps with my cousins.

Alisha sniffed her hamburger and made a face. "My meat smells **funny**," she said.

"That's steak sauce," Great-Uncle Sam said. "It's my special burger recipe. You'll like it."

"No, I won't," Alisha said, frowning. She put her burger back on the serving plate. "I want a **hot dog**."

"I like burgers better," I said.

"So do I," Alisha agreed. "But not with steak sauce."

Jose shook the ketchup bottle. The **ketchup** wouldn't come out. Jose pounded on the bottom of the bottle. The ketchup still wouldn't come out.

He shook the bottle really hard. It came out that time — and splattered all over me!

"Watch it, Jose!" I yelled. I didn't mean to snap. I was just surprised, and upset. My new shirt had red ketchup dots all over it. It looked TERRIBLE. And ketchup leaves stains!

"Claudia yelled at me!" Jose screamed.

"My shirt is ruined," I said.

"Put some cold water on it," **Grandma** said. "I'll take the stains out tomorrow."

I went into the beach house and put cold water on the ketchup spots. **The dots faded a little.**

When I went back outside, I tried to eat. Macaroni  salad kept falling off Gabe's fork. He picked a piece off the sandy step and ate it. He drank his grape juice way too fast. It started to dribble down the sides of his mouth.

I only ate half of my burger and corn. **Watching Gabe killed my appetite.**

Mom and Aunt Maria cleared the table. Everyone was too **full** for dessert. We decided to have it later.

Randi and Mason waved from their porch. "Come on over, Claudia!" Randi called. They were ready to play dominoes.

"Go ahead, Claudia," Mom said.

I **SMILED** and turned to leave.

Then **Mom** said, "**Aren't you forgetting something?**"

"What?" I asked.

"Your cousins," Mom said. "The grownups want to talk. You'll need to take your cousins with you."

Claudia's Not-So-Fabulous Florida Vacation Journal

The Beach House, Florida. Thursday, 7:52 p.m.

Teenagers hate having little kids tag along. Don't my parents know that? Aunt Maria and Uncle Renaldo probably don't care. I almost don't blame them. If I lived with Alisha, Jose, and Gabe, I'd want someone else to watch them, too!

Mason and Randi were surprised to see my cousins. They said it was okay, but they were just being nice.

"You can play dominoes with us," **Mason** told Alisha, "but you have to follow the 𝕽𝖀𝕷𝕰𝕾."

"Okay," **Alisha** said. She smiled sweetly at Mason. I almost fainted. I had never seen Alisha smile before.

"I want to watch cartoons," Jose said.

"Too bad," Randi said. "We're playing dominoes."

Jose stamped his foot. He folded his arms and hung his head. He sniffled. **We all ignored him.**

Randi and Mason sat down at their kitchen table. I started to sit in the chair beside Mason, but Alisha pushed me out of the way. She sat down and **stuck her tongue out** at me.

I sat by Randi. Gabe climbed into my lap.

We each took seven dominoes. I stood my tiles on their sides so I could see what I had.

"Crash!" Gabe yelled. He reached out and knocked my dominoes down. Face up! Everyone saw my tiles.

"Don't do that, Gabe!" I said loudly. I set my tiles on their sides again.

Gabe knocked them down again. Then he piled them up like building blocks.

Jose sat on the steps and BANGED his feet.

"Do you have a nine, Alisha?" Mason asked.

"No," Alisha said, shaking her head.

"Then you have to take another domino," I said. "Now it's my turn."

I looked through my pile of tiles. **Gabe** squirmed on my lap. He kicked my leg when I put a nine down.

"That's **MINE**!" Gabe cried.

"We're supposed to play them, Gabe," I said. "Not just keep them on the table. We have to play them to win."

"I want to watch cartoons!" Jose shrieked.

I put Gabe down and rushed over to Jose. "Be quiet, Jose!" I said. "You're being really **rude**."

"I want to watch cartoons!" Jose squealed.

"Be **QUIET** now," I told him. "I'll let you watch cartoons when we get back to the motel!"

Jose sniffled and wiped his nose on his arm. But at least he stopped screeching.

"Gabe!" Alisha exclaimed.

I looked back at the table. Gabe was giggling and mixing up all the dominoes on the table.

"Now we have to start over," **Randi** said.

"No, I'll just take these guys and go," I said. My cousins were **my problem**. It wasn't fair to ask Randi and Mason to put up with them.

"Thanks a lot, Gabe!" Alisha yelled. She glared at her little brother. "I don't want to leave!"

"Too bad. We're going," I said.

Gabe was 𝕋𝕀ℝ𝔼𝔻 and ℂℝ𝔸ℕ𝕂𝕐. He screamed when I picked him up. I led Jose and Alisha off the deck. Then I turned back to Randi and Mason.

"How late will you guys be up?" I asked.

"Not long," Mason said. "We're getting up early tomorrow to go snorkeling."

"You can come," Randi added. **"But no little kids."**

"I'll be there," I said. "𝔸𝕃𝕆ℕ𝔼."

The kids fell asleep ten minutes after we got back to the beach house. The adults were talking about **boring stuff.** I wanted to go to bed early so I'd be wide awake in the morning.

I went outside to tell my mom I was going back to the motel.

Before I could open my mouth, Grandma smiled at me. She said, "There's my best helper. Let's clean up this mess, Claudia."

Claudia's Not-So-Fabulous Florida Vacation Journal

The Beach House, Florida. Thursday, 9:17 p.m.

The Cortez ship has a bunch of captains, some lazy passengers, and one person who does all the work. Me!

Family Faults

I threw away the *paper plates* and napkins. Grandma took the real dishes inside. I don't mind helping Grandma. **She does a lot for me**. She helps everyone. But nobody else offered to pitch in.

"Where's Jimmy, Grandma?" I asked.

"He went to the arcade with some boys he met on the beach," Grandma said. "I'm glad. Your brother spends too much time ALONE playing games."

I didn't tell Grandma I wanted to be with my new friends, too. It wasn't *her fault* my cousins messed up the domino game, or that everyone was having fun but me.

Then Uncle Diego played "**The Sloop John B**" **on his guitar.** It was an old folk song. All the grown-ups knew the words.

Mom and Dad sat on the steps. Dad had his arm around Mom. They sang and watched the little white waves roll in.

Aunt Maria clapped when Uncle Diego finished. "That was really good," she told him. "Do you play with a band?"

"No," Uncle Diego said. "Then my 𝓗𝓞𝓑𝓑𝓨 would turn into my 𝓙𝓞𝓑. Then maybe singing wouldn't be **fun** anymore."

"I see," Aunt Maria said.

"Let's have a **singalong** one of these nights," **Uncle Diego** suggested. "The kids too."

"Speaking of our kids, they should be in bed," Aunt Maria said.

"They're asleep," Uncle Renaldo pointed out. "If we move them, **they might wake up**."

"They should be asleep in bed," Aunt Maria argued.

I ducked behind the table. I had to hide before Aunt Maria asked me to take her kids back to the motel!

I stayed down and crawled into the house.

Grandma was washing the dishes. I used a small towel to dry them. The beach house doesn't have a dishwasher.

"What's going on out there?" Grandma asked.

I shrugged. **I wasn't in the mood for talking**.

Claudia's Not-So-Fabulous Florida Vacation Journal

Motel Room, Florida. Thursday, 10:37 p.m.

My dad says, "Life isn't fair." Boy, is that true!

People who aren't dependable and mess up never get asked to do anything, because they aren't dependable and they mess up!

That's why nobody asks Jimmy to do anything.

People ask me to babysit and do chores because I always show up and I do a good job.

So bad behavior gets a lot of time off, and good behavior gets a lot of work! That is so wrong.

CHAPTER 5

Friday
Escape

The next morning, I got up at 6:30. Aunt Maria and Uncle Renaldo liked to sleep late. The cousins weren't awake either.

So no one heard me **sneak out**.

I left a note on Mom and Dad's door.

Dear Mom and Dad,

Snorkeling with Randi and Mason.

Buddy system.

Check with Grandma.

Love, Claudia

Next I ran to the beach house. Grandma was already up. She was in the kitchen. Great-Grandpa Cortez, Great-Aunt Louisa, and Great-Uncle Sam were still sleeping.

"You're up EARLY," Grandma said. She  looked at my beach bag. "Going somewhere?"

"Randi and Mason invited me to go snorkeling," I explained. "They're leaving any minute! But Mom and Dad aren't awake. Can I go?"

"Maybe," Grandma said. "Breakfast first."

"Can I have the strawberry shortcake I didn't eat last night?" I asked. "On the porch, please?"

Randi and Mason came over when I sat down on the porch. Grandma gave them strawberry shortcake too. Mason was carrying an extra **boogie board** for me to use.

"Claudia can't go swimming alone," Grandma said.

"There's a lifeguard," Randi said. "And **we watch out** for each other."

"It's called **the buddy system**," I explained.

"You can see Old Boat Reef from here," **Mason** told Grandma. He pointed down the beach. "Mom knows where it is."

"Okay, Claudia," Grandma said. "You can go." She gave each of us a bag of snacks and a bottle of water.

"Be back by 3 o'clock," Grandma said. "We're eating dinner EARLY in case anyone has plans for tonight."

I hugged her. Then Mason, Randi, and I took off down the beach.

Claudia's Maybe-Fabulous Florida Vacation Journal

Seminole Beach, Florida. Friday, 7:19 a.m.

Okay, I have to admit it. I didn't ask Mom and Dad about snorkeling on purpose. I didn't want them to tell me I had to babysit. It's my turn to have fun.

Old Boat Reef

The beach wasn't crowded yet. One man was fishing. A woman jogged by with her dog. Three teenagers were setting up a net for volleyball.

Mason and Randi and I picked a spot to stash our stuff. I had my bathing suit on under my clothes, so I **was ready** to hit the water.

I took off my T-shirt and shorts and looked for my sunscreen. But it wasn't in my bag. **I'd left it at the motel!**

"Randi, do you have any sunscreen?" I asked.

Randi frowned. "I put sunscreen on at home," she said. "I'm sorry!"

"It's okay," I said. "I'm sure **I'll be fine.**"

Then Mason yelled, "Grab your **goggles**, and let's go!" He ran down to the water. He was carrying a net bag for shells.

I'd **snorkeled** before, in the lake back home. But in the lake, there wasn't much to see. The bottom was mucky, and the water was cold and brown. The Florida water was warm and clear.

"Rinse your goggles before you put them on," Mason said. "Then they won't cloud up."

"If you get water in your snorkel," Randi said, "just blow it out."

I got water in my snorkel right away. I didn't blow it out. **I forgot what Randi told me to do.**

I panicked! I swallowed the water and gagged! Sea water is full of salt! *UGH*.

The boogie board made it easy to float. I put my face in the water and paddled. It was like watching underwater TV.

The waves made ripples in the sand. Most of the shells were broken. I saw a starfish and some round brown disks. The water wasn't deep. I dove down and picked up one of the disks.

FYI: (For your information)

1. A long cord is attached to the boogie board.

2. The other end is wrapped around my wrist.

3. The boogie board can't drift away.

I popped back out of the water and showed Mason the disk. "What's this?" I asked. The disk was fuzzy with a hole in the middle. It was flat on one side, and rounded on the other.

"A sand dollar," Mason said. "A live one."

"𝔼𝕎𝕎!" I said. I dropped it. I wanted souvenirs, but I didn't want to kill anything.

Randi laughed. "The white ones are dead," she told me. "Just like the other shells."

Fish were swimming below us. Some were blue and yellow. Others were green and brown. A few had black and white stripes.

We paddled around for an hour. **There was so much to see!** I saw some creatures I'd never seen before, except on TV. Anemones are animals. They look like wiggly spaghetti flowers. **Sea horses** are brown and hard to spot. They blend in with seaweed. Live lobsters are green.

A **barracuda** is long and skinny and has sharp teeth. They're bigger than the other fish. I came face to face with one. **It scared me so much I shrieked!**

"That's Tiger," Randi said. "He finds food around the reef."

"Do **human toes** look like fish food?" I asked.

"Yeah," Mason said, "but Tiger doesn't eat much."

"Stop teasing, Mason!" Randi said, laughing. She splashed her brother. "Tiger won't bother you if you don't bother him, Claudia," she told me.

"Don't worry!" I said. I did not want to tangle with Tiger's teeth.

We dove down to collect some white sand dollars. We even found a few shells that weren't broken. Then we went back to the beach. We rested and ate snacks.

"Want to see something **cool**?" Mason asked.  He broke a **white sand dollar** in half.

I frowned. "Why did you break it?" I asked.

"To show you the little angels inside," Mason said. He shook the broken sand dollar. Tiny pieces fell into my hand. They looked like little wings.

"Wow!" I said. "**That is cool.**"

"We're going to see that new Super Six movie tonight," Mason said. "Do you want to come?"

"Sure!" I said. I love the Super Six. Three of the heroes are girls.

"We'll pick you up at seven," **Mason** said.

"You're such a flirt, Mason," Randi teased.

"I'm not flirting. I'm just being nice," Mason said.

Randi and I buried Mason in the sand. Then we rode waves with our boogie boards and played Frisbee. Suddenly, we realized that it was almost 3 o'clock. We packed our things and headed back.

As I walked toward the motel, **I was filled with dread.** My cousin-free day on the beach was over.

Claudia's Almost-Fabulous Florida Vacation Journal

Seminole Beach, Florida. Friday, 3:07 p.m.

Was Mason flirting with me? Or was he just being nice? Is going to the movies a date? I want to see the Super Six movie on Skull Island, but I don't want to go on a date.

Seminole Beach, Florida. Friday, 3:12 p.m.

I've thought about it. My insides don't feel like mush when I see Mason. I don't stumble over words or choke up when I talk to him.

I just like him as a friend. So going to the movies with Mason and his sister is not a date.

That's a relief! I don't want to feel guilty about having a good time.

Good News

Mom and Dad said I could go to the movies!

Aunt Maria and Uncle Renaldo were taking my cousins to play miniature golf at Pirate's Cove that night.

I didn't have to babysit. I just had to watch the kids for a little while in the afternoon, while Mom and Aunt Maria helped Grandma make dinner.

My cousins were playing on the beach. "Where were you today?" **Alisha** asked.

"I went snorkeling with Randi and Mason," I said.

Alisha kicked sand at me and STOMPED off. She sat down about twenty feet away with her back to me.

I shrugged. I was getting used to Alisha's **weird moods.**

Gabe and I built a **sand castle**.

Jose made a pirate ship with driftwood and seaweed. We used small shells for people. Jose's pirates fought Gabe's soldiers. **We had a blast.**

Alisha just sat and *POUTED*.

After dinner, I waited until the cousins left for Pirate Cove. Then I rushed back to the motel to change.

"Ouch!" I yelled when I took off my T-shirt. My skin was **redder than a boiled lobster!** I hadn't realized how bad my sunburn was.

I took a shower. Even cold water stung my sunburn.

It was only 5:30. I didn't have to go to Randi and Mason's house until 7 o'clock. I stretched out to watch TV for a while.

I must have fallen asleep, because I woke up when the cousins came back.

Alisha pushed me over in the bed. "Move over, Claudia," she said.

I yelled, "Ow!"

I thought I would die! My sunburn hurt so bad!

I gently rolled over and looked at the clock. It was 9:30.

Claudia's Not-So-Fabulous Florida Vacation

Motel Room, Florida. Friday, 9:45 p.m.

I am so mad! I missed going out with my new friends again. And I missed seeing the Super Six movie on Skull Island. And it hurts when I move. Sunburn pain is the worst.

Don't ever forget sunscreen on the beach!

CHAPTER 6

Saturday
Pirate Parade

When I woke up on Saturday morning, Jose and **Gabe** were already awake.

"Hurry up, Claudia!" **Jose** said. "We're going to miss the Pirate Parade if you don't get up and get ready now!"

"Okay, okay," I said. I got dressed. Then my cousins and I met Uncle Diego outside.

The Pirate Parade was going to go right past the motel. We sat on a bench and waited. Soon, Randi and Mason walked up and sat down next to me.

Randi noticed my long sleeves and jeans. "Aren't you hot?" she asked.

"Yeah, but I have a really bad sunburn," I explained. I felt stupid. It was really hot outside already, and getting hotter. But I didn't want to make my sunburn worse!

"Is this a REAL pirate parade?" Jose asked.

"There aren't any real pirates," Alisha answered. "Only FAKE ones."

"But they throw **beads** and stuff," Mason explained. "It's like pirate treasure."

"Wow!" Jose yelled. He looked **really excited**.

Uncle Diego yawned. He never gets excited.

"Pirates!" Gabe shouted. He clapped his chubby hands.

"Pirates are silly," **Alisha** said. "But I like beads."

"Here they come!" Randi told Gabe. She pointed down the street.

The first car in the parade was decorated with pirate flags and fake parrots. Two ladies threw strings of plastic silver beads toward us. We all reached to catch one, but only Mason got one of the necklaces.

Alisha held up her hand. "Can I have it?" she asked, smiling sweetly.

"Sure," **Mason** said. He gave her the beads.

"𝕄𝕀ℕ𝔼!" Gabe yelled, grabbing for the necklace.

"You can have the next one, Gabe," I said.

Randi waved at the next float. "Over here!" she called.

The second car was pulling a trailer with **palm trees, parrots, and treasure chests.** Teenagers dressed like pirates and colonial ladies were riding on the float. They threw red and green beads.

Randi, Mason, and I each caught one. We gave the beads to the cousins.

I took Gabe's hand so he wouldn't run away. He wanted more beads, but catching them wasn't easy.

"Blue!" Gabe shouted. He jumped up and down and pulled on my arm. "Get them!"

A man threw a string of blue beads right at me. I caught them. "Thank you!" I called to him.

"I want blue ones," **Alisha** said. I looked at her. She was wearing 𝔹𝕌ℕℂℍ𝔼𝕊 of beads. She had silver, gold, red, and green necklaces.

"*You can't have mine!*" Jose told her. He was wearing four blue strands.

"I'll trade you three silver for one blue," Alisha said.

"No," Jose yelled. He ducked between two adults. Then he caught a necklace with a big **gold coin** attached to one end.

"I want one of those!" Alisha yelled. She stepped off the curb. She jumped up and down and shouted at the float. "Me! Me!" she called.

Another gold coin necklace sailed through the air.

Alisha jumped, but an older boy jumped higher. He caught it and gave it to his little sister.

"That was mine!" Alisha screeched. "He took my beads!"

"**Quiet, Alisha!**" Mason snapped.

Alisha shut up. Her lip **quivered**, and tears rolled down her face. I could tell that she was **embarrassed**.

Mason felt terrible. He put his arm around Alisha and said, "I have beads just like that at home. I'll give them to you later."

"Okay," Alisha said, sniffling quietly.

Then Jose and Gabe ran past me into the street. "Money!" Gabe yelled. They both picked up candy wrapped in gold foil. I bent down and scooped up six chocolate coins.

Jose reached for the last coin. Another boy reached at the same time. They bumped heads, and they both cried. Then Alisha picked up the coin. **That made the boys cry harder.**

I gave three of my gold coins to Jose and three to the other boy.

"Hey! I only got one!" Alisha said. She kicked me.

Claudia's Sort-of Fabulous Florida Vacation Journal

Gulf Avenue, Florida. Saturday, 11:45 a.m.

Little kids are a lot like pirates.

1. They want gold, silver, and jewels.

2. No matter how much they have, they want more.

3. They don't like to share.

4. They punish people who make them mad.

There's only one difference:

Pirates made people walk the plank.

Little kids throw screaming fits and kick shins.

I don't know which is worse.

Beware

MOTEL

After the parade, we took the cousins back to the **motel**. Randi and Mason came too. The kids ran ahead. They wanted to show Aunt Maria and Uncle Renaldo their beads.

"Why do you have to babysit so much?" Randi asked.

"I'm here, and my aunt and uncle **trust me**," I said.

"Do they pay you?" Mason asked.

"No," I said, shaking my head.

"That's not fair," Mason said.

Randi agreed. "You're a kid too," she told me.

"We want to hang out with you," Mason said. "Not with **your cousins**."

"They're a little ẞRẞTTY," Randi said quietly.

I knew she was right. "They're going swimming with their parents this afternoon," I said. "I can't because I'm sunburned."

"Great!" Mason said. "Come over to our house later. We'll watch a movie."

They headed home, and I headed into the motel. My aunt and uncle were still asleep.

I turned on **cartoons**. I couldn't leave my cousins alone, so I was babysitting again.

For free.

I was asked to do a lot of things because I was dependable.

1. I'm the only person who feeds Ping-Ping or cleans her litter box. Even though Mom and Dad have had her since before I was born.

2. At home, I have to do the dishes. Jimmy doesn't rinse them well enough.

3. Kids at school always want me as a project partner. I'll do all the work to make sure I get an A.

I was sick of it.

Claudia's Awful Florida Vacation Journal

Motel Room, Florida. Saturday, 12:23 p.m.

Uncle Diego once said that desperate times called for desperate measures. That means that when things are really bad, you might have to do things you wouldn't normally do. Well, I'm desperate!

Plus, cartoon music is driving me nuts!

Desperate Measures

Desperate Measure #1: Hide

After my cousins went to the beach, I went to see Randi and Mason. I didn't leave a note, and I didn't tell anyone. **I wouldn't have to do anything if nobody could find me!**

That worked great for two hours. We ate snacks and watched a movie.

"Your parents invited us to your great-grandfather's birthday party tomorrow," Randi said.

"It'll be better than the FIREWORKS on the beach tonight," Mason said.

"Which you're coming to with us, right?" Randi asked. "They start at dark."

"Okay!" I told her. I smiled. Fireworks sounded fun!

Just then, someone pounded at the front door. Mason opened it. My dad was standing there, and he looked mad.

I got up, said good-bye to Mason and Randi, and left. My dad and I walked toward the beach house.

"I've been looking all over for you," **Dad** said. "Why didn't you leave a note? Or tell someone where you were? Your mother is *very worried*."

I shrugged. "Randi and Mason invited me over," I told him.

"At least you're all right," Dad said. He sighed. "Jimmy cut his finger helping Grandma with the dishes. **Your mom has not had a good afternoon.**"

"Sorry," I muttered. I was SORRY I made my parents NERVOUS. I was SORRY that Grandma always got stuck doing dishes. I was not sorry that Jimmy had to clean up after lunch.

"Your mom and I are going to dinner with Renaldo and Maria," Dad said. "You can have **pizza** with your cousins."

I gasped. I couldn't believe it. "I have to babysit again?" I asked quietly.

Desperate Measure #2: Just Say No

"At 6 o'clock," Dad said. "For a couple hours."

"I can't!" I said. "I promised to watch the fireworks with Randi and Mason."

"We'll be back before dark," Dad said.

Trying to say no didn't work, but I wasn't ready to give up.

At the beach house, Aunt Maria was sitting under a beach umbrella, reading a magazine.

"Did you have to work on your school vacations when you were in seventh grade, Aunt Maria?" I asked.

"Of course not!" **Aunt Maria** said, smiling. **"It's not a vacation if you have to work."**

"Exactly!" I exclaimed. "I bet Alisha and Jose and Gabe would love to go out to dinner with you," I added.

"Nope. They want to have pizza with you," Aunt Maria said.

"What if I have other plans?" I asked quietly.

Aunt Maria looked up from her magazine. "What? Did you say something?" she asked.

"At home, Mom pays me **two dollars** an hour to watch the little boy who lives next door to us," I said.

"Well, that's nice of her," Aunt Maria said. **She did not offer to pay me.**

I SIGHED. Then I went inside the beach house.

"Why can't Great-Aunt Louisa and Great-Uncle Sam watch the cousins, Grandma?" I asked.

"They'll probably **fall asleep**," **Grandma** explained.

"Can't you do it?" I asked.

"I have to take care of Great-Grandpa," Grandma said. "I'm sorry, but you have to watch your cousins, Claudia."

Desperate Measure #3: No Show

I had to do something. If I didn't, I never would.

I went walking on the beach at 5:30.

I came back to the motel at 6:45.

Dad was sitting on a bench when I walked up to the motel. He looked **MAD** when he saw me. I hated making Dad mad. *He never yelled.* He calmly told me my punishment. Then he wouldn't talk to me until it was over.

Dad pointed to the bench. I sat down.

"We had a reservation at a very nice restaurant," Dad said. "Your mother really wanted to eat there, but it's **too late** now."

I looked at the ground. I didn't try to explain. I didn't have an excuse. *I had been late on purpose.*

"We'll have to eat somewhere else," Dad said. "We're taking your cousins with us. You can't be trusted."

I smiled. **Messing up worked!** I didn't have to watch my cousins after all.

But Dad wasn't finished. "You're GROUNDED for the rest of our vacation," he told me. No **fireworks** and no **birthday party**. And no hanging out with Mason and Randi."

Claudia's Worst Vacation Ever Journal

Motel Room, Florida. Saturday, 7:18 p.m.

I'm not dependable anymore. So I guess nobody will ask me to do stuff. That's what I wanted, but I don't feel like I won. I feel like a total loser.

CHAPTER 7

Sunday
Breakfast Blues

My fabulous Florida vacation was RUINED.

That night, I watched the **fireworks** from the motel window. ALONE. My cousins weren't even there. But they were at the beach house the next day to bug me at breakfast.

"Claudia's in trouble!" Alisha sang, skipping around me. "Claudia's in trouble."

Gabe put a **huge beetle** in my cereal.

Jose tripped over my foot. Then he said I tried to hurt him on purpose.

After breakfast, I picked up Jimmy's **video game.** I usually didn't play video games, but I was **bored.** Dad took it away.

A few minutes later, Randi and Mason stopped by. "Want to go snorkeling again?" Mason asked.

"Can't." I said. I didn't want to explain.

Alisha explained for me. "Claudia's **grounded**," she said. Then she shut the door.

I volunteered to help **Grandma** with the dishes. I needed her advice. **So I was honest.**

"I was late on purpose," I confessed.

"Why?" Grandma asked. She wasn't mad. She was puzzled.

I looked down at the ground. Then I said, "Everybody expects me to babysit and help out. Even if I don't want to or I have something else to do. I don't even get paid. Aunt Maria and Uncle Renaldo stick me with the cousins **just because I'm there** and they want to sleep."

I took a quick breath. Then I went on, "**Jimmy** doesn't have to do anything. Plus, he doesn't get grounded when he *messes up*, which is all the time."

"Did you tell your father that?" Grandma asked.

I shook my head. I knew that Dad wouldn't take back a punishment unless he was wrong. *He wasn't wrong.* I was late on purpose.

"Your dad deserves an explanation," Grandma said.

I sighed. "Okay," I said.

"And you should be nicer to Alisha," Grandma added.

"No way!" I exclaimed. "She's a selfish brat, and she hates me."

"No, she doesn't," Grandma said. She patted my cheek.

Claudia's Still-Awful Florida Vacation Journal

Motel Room, Florida. Sunday, 11:47 a.m.

Grandma said that Alisha picks on me because she wants me to like her. Really! Grandma said that Alisha thinks I won't like her, so she does awful things to make sure of it. That way her feelings won't be hurt.

It makes sense in a weird seven-year-old way. Alisha can tell herself it's the awful things I don't like, not her.

Fixing a Problem

I found Mom and Dad and told them everything.

"I'm on vacation too," I explained. "But nobody else had to babysit or help Grandma clean up."

Dad didn't say anything. He **raised an eyebrow.** He does that when something seems odd or unbelievable. So do I.

"**Taking you for granted** wasn't fair," Mom said. "But you should have told us before you got into trouble. It's too late now."

"I know," I said. "**I'm really sorry** I made you miss dinner at that nice restaurant."

I went back to the motel room. I read another chapter of my 𝔹𝕆𝕆𝕂. I didn't fall asleep.

Claudia's Not-So-Terrible Florida Vacation Journal

Motel Room, Florida. Sunday, 2:11 p.m.

Nobody can fix a problem if they don't know there is a problem.

Mom and Dad didn't realize they were being unfair. I didn't tell them. I just did something mean to hurt them.

Afternoon Apologies

Being grounded at the beach was **a hundred times worse** than being grounded at home.

The whole Gulf of Mexico was right outside, but I couldn't even get my big toe wet.

I couldn't even watch a movie on TV.

Jose was watching cartoons. And I was watching the cousins.

Dad knew I wouldn't do anything STUPID like leave the kids alone. He was right. **I wanted him to trust me again.**

The **Claudia Cristina Cortez Rebellion** was over.

"Would you like me to fix your hair, Alisha?" I asked. "For the party tonight?"

Grandma told me that **Alisha** would stop being a brat if I was nice to her. I didn't think it would work, but it was worth a shot.

Alisha frowned. "Fix it how?" she asked suspiciously.

"Make it curly like mine," I said. "And tie it with a ribbon. I have lots of different colors."

Alisha scrunched up her face. "Okay, but it better not hurt," she said finally.

"It won't," I said.

Alisha sat in a chair. I used my curling iron to curl her hair. I was very careful so that I wouldn't burn her.

When the curls were done, I pulled her hair back into a ponytail. Then I tied a ribbon around it. The pink ribbon matched her shirt.

"You look GREAT!" I exclaimed.

Alisha nodded, but she didn't look happy.

I pretended not to notice. "Let's do your nails too," I said.

First, I soaked her fingers in soapy water. Then I filed the rough edges of her nails.

While I filed her nails, I talked about the teen magazines I liked. But Alisha didn't say anything.

I was starting to think that Grandma had been **really, really wrong** about Alisha.

"Pick a color," I said. I showed her three bottles of **fingernail polish.**

Alisha suddenly glared at me. "Do you think Mason is cute?" she asked.

"Yeah," I said. "But he's not as cute as **Brad Turino**."

"Who's Brad Turino?" Alisha asked.

"He's the boy I like at school," I said.

"You have a BOYFRIEND?" Alisha whispered. She stopped glaring.

Then I figured something out.

Alisha had a crush on Mason! She was jealous of me because she thought I liked Mason too.

That's why she was acting like a total brat!

But she wouldn't be jealous if she knew I liked someone else.

"He's not my boyfriend, but I wish he was," I said. "He's a fantastic **football** player, and he's totally GORGEOUS."

"Cool!" Alisha said. She grinned. Then she pointed to the pink nail polish. "I like that one the best," she told me.

I painted Alisha's nails very carefully. While I did, she talked about how FUNNY and cool Mason was.

"Let's put on a little bit of lip gloss," I said. "I wiped off the Gabe germs."

Alisha giggled. Then she hugged me. "Thanks, Claudia," she said. "I wish you could come to Great-Grandpa's party."

"Me too," I told her.

The cousins left for the party at 5:30.

I changed the TV channel at 5:31. Cartoon music was giving me a headache.

Then **Dad** came to the door. "**I owe you an apology, Claudia,**" he said. "It was wrong to make you work so much on your vacation."

I blinked with surprise.

"That doesn't excuse what you did," he went on. "You were late on purpose. So **you still have to be punished.** But you can be grounded when we get home. You should enjoy the rest of your vacation."

I almost fell over!

Claudia's Fabulous Florida Vacation Journal

Motel Room, Florida. Sunday, 5:36 p.m.

I'm going to Great—Grandpa's birthday party!

CHAPTER 8

P.S.

Great-Grandpa Cortez's party was awesome. Uncle Renaldo and Aunt Maria helped Mom cook and clean up. That meant that Grandma got to relax for a change.

I had a blast.

Dad wasn't mad at me anymore, and Mason and Randi were at the party too. We hung out all night.

Dad told Aunt Maria and Uncle Renaldo they had to pay me two dollars an hour to babysit.

That's a 𝔹𝔸ℝ𝔾𝔸𝕀ℕ, but they grumbled anyway. I guess they thought cousins were 𝔽𝕌ℕ to babysit so they didn't need to pay me.

Uncle Diego played the guitar, and the whole family, plus Mason and Randi, had a singalong on the beach. Jimmy used pots and pans for drums.

Alisha and I are friends now. **Mason** danced with her three times. She was so thrilled she practically **glowed in the dark!**

Mason and **Randi** gave me their e-mail addresses. They want to come visit me on their next vacation! I had the best time with them in Florida. I can't wait until they come to visit me.

Ping-Ping was glad to be home from the vet, but she wouldn't let me pet her for three days. I guess she was still mad at me.

I was glad to be home too, but I'll NEVER **forget** my **fabulous** Florida vacation!

About the Author

Diana G. Gallagher lives in Florida with her husband and five dogs, four cats, and a cranky parrot. Her hobbies are gardening, garage sales, and grandchildren. She has been an English equitation instructor, a professional folk musician, and an artist. However, she had aspirations to be a professional writer at the age of twelve. She has written dozens of books for kids and young adults.

About the Illustrator

Brann Garvey lives in Minneapolis, Minnesota with his wife, Keegan, and their very fat cat, Iggy. Brann graduated from Iowa State University with a bachelor of fine arts degree. He later attended the Minneapolis College of Art and Design, where he studied illustration. In his free time, Brann enjoys being with his family and friends. He brings his sketchbook everywhere he goes.

Glossary

appetite (AP-uh-tite)—desire for food

behavior (bi-HAYV-yur)—the way that a person acts or speaks

chaos (KAY-oss)—total confusion

dependable (di-PEND-uh-buhl)—if you are dependable, people rely on you and count on you

desperate (DESS-pur-it)—if you are desperate, you will do anything to change your situation

dominoes (DOM-uh-nohz)—a game played with small, rectangular tiles. The tiles are divided into two halves that are blank or contain dots.

goggles (GOG-uhlz)—special glasses that fit tightly around your eyes to protect them

parched (PARCHD)—if you are parched, you are very thirsty

snorkel (SNOR-kuhl)—a tube that you use to breathe through when you are **snorkeling**, which is swimming underwater

souvenir (soo-vuh-NEER)—an object you keep to remind you of a special person, event, or place

Discussion Questions

1. Did Claudia do the right thing when she didn't show up to babysit? What would you have done? What else could she have done?

2. Claudia is forced to babysit her three cousins in this book. What is a chore that you have to do?

3. Why does Claudia have to use the buddy system when she goes swimming in the ocean?

Writing Prompts

1. Great-Grandpa Cortez is the oldest person in Claudia's family. Who is the oldest person in your family? Write about that person.

2. Have you ever gone on vacation with your family? Where did you go? If you haven't gone on a vacation, write about a place where you'd like to travel one day!

3. Claudia meets two friends in Florida. Do you have any friends or relatives who don't live near you? Write about them.

MORE FUN
with Claudia!

Claudia Cristina Cortez

Just like every other thirteen-year-old girl, Claudia Cristina Cortez has a complicated life. Whether she's studying for the big Quiz Show, babysitting her neighbor, Nick, avoiding mean Jenny Pinski, planning the seventh-grade dance, or trying desperately to pass the swimming test at camp, Claudia goes through her complicated life with confidence, cleverness, and a serious dash of cool.

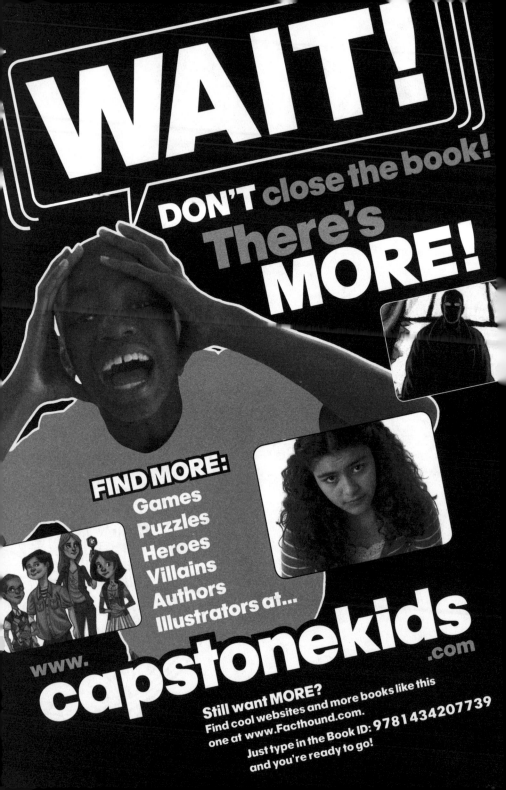